Little Bear's New Friend

Muriel Pépin
Adapted by Deborah Kovacs
Illustrations by Marcelle Geneste

Reader's Digest Young Families, Inc.

The bear family was getting ready for their long winter nap. But the littlest bear cub wasn't feeling a bit sleepy.

"I don't want to stay inside, Mama," he said. "This is such a little cave. I'll be bored staying inside all winter long."

"Dear little bear!" said Mother Bear. "You won't be bored. You'll be asleep. Bears spend the winter sleeping."

So the little bear cub curled up with his family in the snug cave. But when the others began to snore, the little bear cub's eyes were still wide open. As he gazed outside the cave, the first snowflakes of winter drifted gently to the ground.

"It's snowing!" he cried, watching the fluffy flakes pile up on the ground. He had heard about snow, but he had never seen it for himself. The little bear cub had to investigate. Quietly, he crept outside.

"Br-r-r-r! This snow is COLD!" said the little bear cub, patting it with his furry paws. "And it's so WHITE!" He had to blink his eyes to get used to the brightness. "And it's so BEAUTIFUL!" The little bear cub ran through the meadow at full speed, delighted with the swirling white flakes all around him. Then he began to roll, over and over again, in the soft new snow.

Before long, the little bear cub had run and jumped and twirled and spun around so much that he didn't know where his cave was anymore. "Mama!" he cried. "I'm lost!"

"I'll help you," said a voice. The little bear cub looked up and saw a friendly little wolf pup. "We'll find your cave lickety-split. But let's play tag first."

"Okay!" said the little bear cub. "Try to catch me!"

The wolf pup and the bear cub played in the snow for a long time. The wolf pup showed the bear cub how to slide down the slippery hill. The bear cub taught the wolf pup how to slide across the frozen pond. Together, they made pictures of themselves by lying in the snow.

The little bear cub was having such a good time that he forgot all about finding his cave and going back to his mother.

But Mother Bear had not forgotten about her little cub. She woke up and noticed that he was missing. "Where is my little bear?" she worried, hurrying into the forest to find him. "These woods are full of danger. He could get into trouble!" Just then, who should appear but a wolf!

The bear had surprised the wolf, too. They both bared their teeth and started to growl at one another. Then they heard footsteps. Two hunters! Quickly, the animals ran to hide behind a big rock.

When the hunters were gone, Mother Bear turned to the wolf. No longer frightened, she said, "I'm looking for my little cub. I'm afraid he sneaked out this morning to play in the snow."

"So did my little pup," said Mother Wolf, glancing after the hunters. "And I'm worried about him. Let's hurry and find them."

Immediately, the two mothers set out to search the snowy woods. Together they worked much faster than they could have on their own.

"Look!" said Mother Wolf. "My little pup's pawprints!"

"I see my little cub's pawprints, too!" said Mother Bear.

Mother Bear and Mother Wolf followed the tracks—over rocks and stones, climbing up and down—right to the bears' den. Slowly they approached the entrance, their hearts pounding, and there they discovered an astonishing sight.

Inside the den they saw the little gray wolf pup sound asleep, snuggled in a pile of snoring bear cubs.

"It looks as if my little bear has found a new friend," said Mother Bear happily.

"And my little wolf has found the coziest place in the forest for a midwinter nap!" replied Mother Wolf.

When a bear cub is born, it is small enough to fit in your hand. Cubs live with their mother for two years, and she teaches them everything they need to know to live on their own. Bear cubs grow quickly— an adult stands almost seven feet high!

Bears are very powerful animals. They move heavy rocks to eat the insects hiding underneath and can even split old tree trunks when looking for food.

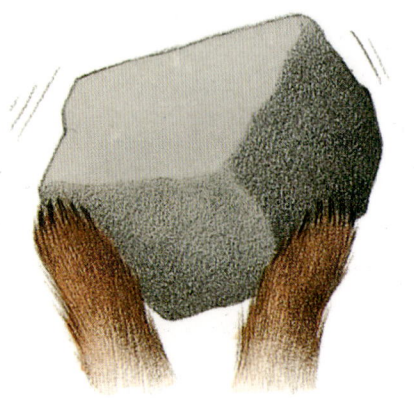

Bears are great tree climbers. They shake a branch so that the nuts and fruits fall to the ground, then scramble down for a feast.